Robbie Reader

Meeting my CASA

First published by Robe Communications, 2009

ISBN: 978-0-9817403-5-5

Printed in the United States of America

www.robbietherabbit.com

A special thanks goes to...

Dan Prater, at CASA of Southwest Missouri,
for his valuable input.

* * * * * * * * * * * * * * * * * * *

Check out these other great
Robbie Rabbit™ books!

Moving to another Foster Home, a Robbie Reader™

Wanting to Belong, a Robbie Reader™

Robbie's Trail through Foster Care
An Adult Guide to Robbie's Trail through Foster Care

Robbie's Trail through Adoption
An Adult Guide to Robbie's Trail through Adoption

"Doorbell!" called Robbie, slurping another spoonful of carrot soup.

"It must be Kelly!" called Rita, his foster mother, as she scooted off her chair and trotted to the front door.

"Who's Kelly?" wondered Robbie. He suddenly felt nervous — like he'd swallowed a jar of flutterflies. Whenever someone new showed up, it usually meant something was going to change for him. Sometimes he'd get a new therapist or a new caseworker. Other times, he'd have to go to a new foster home.

He could hear Rita at the front door, warning Kelly not to bump her head as she came in.

"Hi, you must be Robbie," announced the giraffe. "I'm Kelly — your new CASA."

"Uh, hi," Robbie said quietly. He swiped his carrot mustache with his paw.

"Do you know what a CASA is?" she asked.

"Isn't it a house?" he asked shyly.

Kelly smiled. "Well, if you spoke Spanish, it could mean house. But when I say I'm your CASA, it means that I'm your *Court-Appointed Special Advocate*."

"You're a pointed special what?" he asked.

"CASA stands for *Court-Appointed Special Advocate*. CASAs watch out for animals in foster care and then tell other animals — like the judge — how you are doing and what you need."

Sounds like what my caseworker and therapist do," Robbie said.

nd of... but CASAs are different. For starters, your case-rker and therapist have a lot of different children they p. Most CASAs work with only one or two special animals at a time," Kelly explained.

"So what you're saying is that a CASA is someone who *Cares about A Special Animal!*" Robbie exclaimed.

"Exactly!" Kelly smiled.

"Judges need each CASA to tell them how animals in foster care are doing," Kelly said. "This helps them make good decisions about what is best for that animal."

"So if I don't like my new school or something, you'll tell the judge?"

"Sure, that's one thing that I'd talk about," Kelly smiled. "I also make sure the adults around you are doing what is best for you while you're in foster care."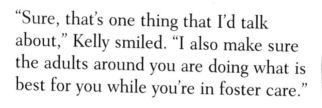

"How do you do that?" Robbie asked.

"I'll talk with them about what they do to help you and your mom," Kelly explained.

"I'll talk with your foster parents, your therapist, teachers, doctors and caseworker — anyone who spends time with you. But most importantly, I spend time with *you* to find out how *you* think things are going."

"It sure sounds like you do a lot of talking," Robbie said. "Does your voice ever hurt?"

Kelly laughed. "Sometimes my throat does hurt because I talk so much. But you know what? If it means that I can make sure you get everything you need, I think it's worth it to get a sore throat every now and then. Don't you agree?"

"Yeah," Robbie said happily.

"After I talk with everyone, I tell the judge what I've learned and suggest anything that might help you."

But my therapist and my caseworker already do that," said Robbie. "Even my foster parents talk at court."

"True… kind of… but none of these animals do exactly what I'll do," Kelly explained. "You've lived in a lot of foster homes, haven't you?"

Robbie nodded.

"And Rita told me that you just got another therapist, too, right?" Kelly prompted.

"Yeah," said Robbie.

"Well, my furry little friend, I'm afraid you're stuck with me. Even if you move to a new foster home or get a new caseworker, I'll still be your CASA," Kelly explained. "Because I'm a CASA, I'll pretty much stick around until your life settles back down."

"Really?"

"Yes, really!" Kelly smiled. "I'll come see you a few times each month. Sometimes I might bring carrot ice cream. Other times, we might play ball together if you want, or we can just sit on your front porch. I'm excited about getting to know you and becoming friends."

obbie smiled.

n fact, I'd like to get started now. Is that OK with you?"

Vell, if you feel like talking," he grinned. They both
arted laughing.

think we'll get along just fine, Robbie."

Start here!

Tell me what you ate for dinner last night. Give a big "thumbs up" or a "thumbs down."

Name one thing you did for fun with a foster parent today or yesterday.

Your tail was caught in a bush. Run in a circle three times while hopping on one foot.

A porcupine bumped into you on accident. You're covered in sharp quills. Who would you ask for help?

You fell into Groundhog's hole. Go back two spaces.

You have one minute to tell me about something nice that a foster parent did for you recently.

Tell me about a time when you were sad because someone didn't keep a promise.

A skunk ran by and it really smells. Move ahead one space.

You have one minute to name three of your friends and to tell me what you like to do with them.

You have one minute to grab something you wrote, drew, colored or made. Tell why you like it.

You have one minute to tell me about a time when you got into trouble. What happened?

A Special Note from Robbie Rabbit

n't it nice to know there are so many people looking out for you? Not all ildren in foster care have CASAs, but they do have guardians ad litem. ASAs and guardians ad litem make sure you get everything you need to be iccessful while you are in foster care.

njoy my time with Kelly (my CASA), because she really listens to me. th all adults that I meet for the first time, I have a hard time knowing at I can tell them and what I shouldn't tell them. But I know I can trust lly. She only makes promises to me that she can keep, and she's always en honest with me. She also spends her time asking me how I am doing, t just asking other adults. This makes me feel important!

nen we get together, she sometimes plays a game with me. Do you want play, too? You'll need 4 Popsicle® sticks, 4 bottle lids (from water or da pop bottles); tape; scissors; and a game die.

ake your game pieces. Get your CASA, caseworker or foster parents — u need someone to help you prepare the game pieces and to play the game with you! Cut out the faces below and tape each onto a Popsicle® stick. Then, have an adult cut a slit into each bottle cap. Slide each stick into a bottle cap just slightly and tape it into place. Ta da! Your game pieces are ready!

How to play. Youngest player goes first. Roll the die and move that many spaces on the board. First one to the playground wins. Have fun!

Your friend, Robbie

CPSIA information can be obtained
at www.ICGtesting.com
228318LV00001B

9780981740355